MEET MARIO!

by Malcolm Shealy

First published in the United States 2021 by Random House Children's Books
This edition published in Great Britain 2023 by Farshore

An imprint of HarperCollins*Publishers*
1 London Bridge Street, London SE1 9GF
www.farshore.co.uk

HarperCollins*Publishers*
Macken House, 39/40 Mayor Street Upper, Dublin 1, D01 C9W8, Ireland

TM & © 2023 Nintendo. All rights reserved.

ISBN 978 0 00 864146 7
Printed in the UK
001

Farshore takes its responsibility to the planet and its inhabitants very seriously. We aim to use papers from well-managed forests run by responsible suppliers.

This book is produced from independently certified FSC™ paper
to ensure responsible forest management.

For more information visit: www.harpercollins.co.uk/green

Reading Together

Before you start reading, talk about what might happen in the story.

Are there any clues on the cover?
Have you seen these characters before?
What do you think this book will be about?
Does the title help you?

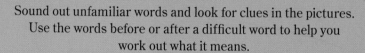

Sound out unfamiliar words and look for clues in the pictures.
Use the words before or after a difficult word to help you
work out what it means.

After you've finished the story, go back to any words
that you found tricky and talk about what they mean.
This helps you remember them!

Activities for After Reading

Can you spot these challenging words in this story?

Citizens   Disturbance   Energetic   Mysterious
Monstrous   Devoted   Mischievous

What does each word mean? How do you know? Does the sentence help?
Can you put the word into another sentence? What kinds of adventures do
you think Mario, Luigi and their friends will have?

Question Time!

What is Donkey Kong's favourite food?
What place is Daisy the princess of?
Who can be counted on to save the day?

Advanced Questions

Which of Mario's friends would NOT be
a good choice to help defeat a ghost? Why?
Which of the characters would you most like to meet?
Which would you least like to meet? Why?

MARIO

Here We Go!

Mario is a cheerful person
who is no stranger to adventure
in the Mushroom Kingdom.
The Mushroom Kingdom
is a peaceful place.
But when there's trouble,
Mario can be counted on
to save the day!

LUIGI

Okey Dokey!

Luigi is Mario's
friendly brother.
Luigi tries to be brave,
but he is timid –
and afraid of ghosts!
Even so, he is willing
to join his brother on
any adventure.

DONKEY KONG

Going Bananas!

Donkey Kong is known
for his great strength
and red tie.
Bananas are Donkey
Kong's favourite food.

YOSHI

Big Appetite! GULP!

Yoshi is laid-back
and likes to eat fruit.
He helps Mario
by using his long tongue
to gobble up enemies.
He can flutter his legs
to jump really high
and avoid danger.

Toad Time!

Toad is one of the citizens
of the Mushroom Kingdom.
He is loyal, cheerful,
and polite.
He's always happy to help
Princess Peach
whenever he's needed.

PRINCESS PEACH

Perfectly Peachy

Peach is the princess of
the Mushroom Kingdom.
She tries many things,
including adventuring,
sports, and kart racing.

DAISY

Princess Power

Daisy is the princess
of Sarasaland.
She is full of energy.
She also enjoys playing
sports and kart racing.

ROSALINA

Mysterious Friend

The mysterious Rosalina
came from outer space with
little Luma, the lost star child.
With her powerful star wand,
Rosalina is always calm
in the face of danger.

TOADETTE

Happy and Hardworking

Toadette lives in the Mushroom Kingdom. She is brave and always ready for adventure.

BOWSER

KING KOOPA

Mario's biggest and baddest
foe is Bowser.
With his pointy horns,
his fiery red hair,
and the spiky shell on his back,
Bowser is also the mighty
King Koopa!

BOWSER Jr.

Like Father, Like Son

Bowser Jr. is Bowser's energetic son.
He wears a bandana painted
to look like a monstrous mouth.
He thinks it makes him look older!
Bowser Jr. is mischievous
and more than a little naughty.

KOOPALINGS

The Koopa Crew

Armed with magic wands and other powerful weapons, the Koopalings are trusted and devoted helpers of Bowser.

Wendy

Lemmy

Morton

Iggy

Roy

Larry

Ludwig

Their names are Lemmy, Wendy,
Morton, Iggy, Roy, Ludwig, and Larry.
Wherever there's a disturbance,
the Koopalings are
almost always involved!

MINIONS

Mighty Minions!

Only Bowser's mighty minions stand between him and Mario. Bowser's minions can be found everywhere – marching in fields, hiding in pipes, and even swimming underwater!

Koopa Troopa

Spiny

Kamek

Piranha Plant

Lakitu

Goomba

Bowser may be a lot of trouble,

but Mario's friends

gain courage

and stand up to Bowser

when they hear

Mario say . . .